This book

belongs to

_____

_____

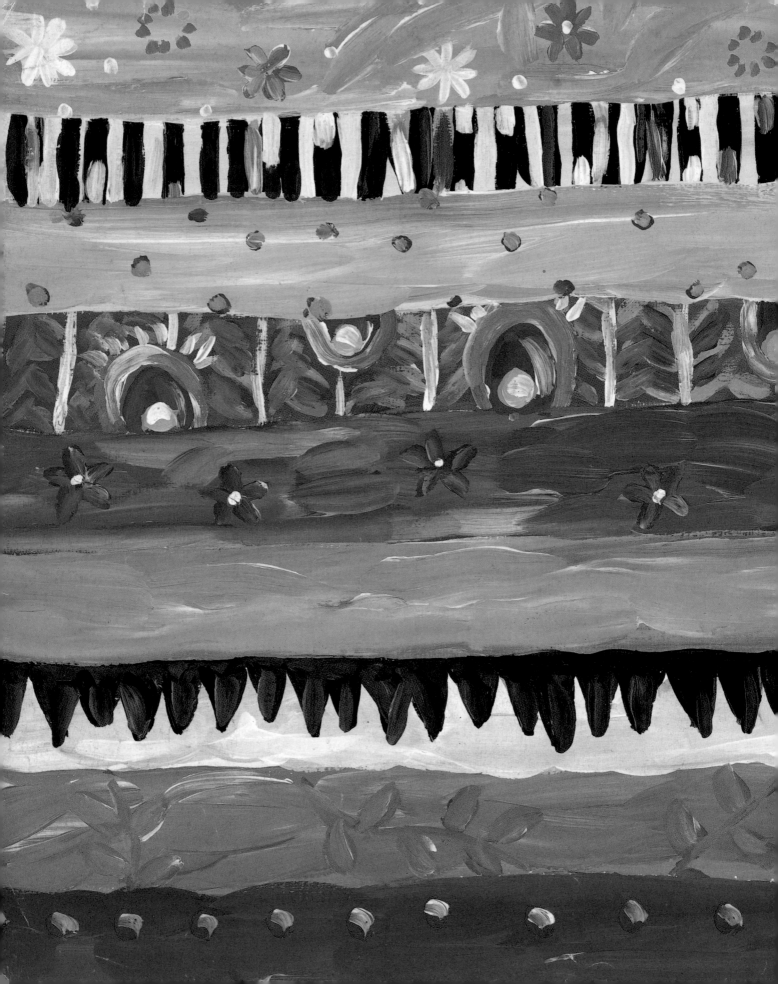

for Meg love J.C.

First published in Great Britain in 2007 by Gullane Children's Books
This edition published in 2008 by

Gullane Children's Books

185 Fleet Street, London EC4A 2HS

3   5   7   9   10   8   6   4

Text and illustrations © Jane Cabrera 2007

ISBN: 978-1-86233-709-1

Printed and bound in china

Cat's Cuddles

Jane Cabrera

GULLANE
CHILDREN'S BOOKS

I love having cuddles!
But who is my favourite
friend to cuddle?

Is it Tiny Mouse

With his teeny,
weeny cuddle?

Is it
Feathery
Peacock

with his bright,
tickly cuddle?

Is it Big Bear
With his cosy,
fluffy cuddle?

Is it Happy
Frog
With her squidgy,
quidgy cuddle?

Is it Cheeky
Monkey
With her tight,
treetop cuddle?

Is it Enormous
Elephant
With his big,
strong cuddle?

Is it Soggy Octopus
with his snug,
squeezy cuddle?

Is it Scaly Armadillo with her safe, friendly cuddle?

Or is it
someone
very special

With the softest, warmest cuddle . . .

Yes!
It's my new
baby brother!

More books from
Jane Cabrera
for you to enjoy

Mummy Carry Me Please!
●
Eggday
written by Joyce Dunbar
_____

Sing-along rhymes

The Wheels On the Bus
●
**Here We Go Round
the Mulberry Bush**
●
One, Two, Buckle My Shoe
●
Old MacDonald Had a Farm
●
Ten in the Bed
●
If You're Happy and You Know It!
●
Old Mother Hubbard
●
Over in the Meadow